The Enchanted Kingdom

STORY BY KAREN SHERMAN-LAVIN
ILLUSTRATIONS BY ALISHA SICKLER-BRUNELLI

ISBN: Softcover   978-1-4990-4438-6
        Hardcover   978-1-4990-4437-9
        EBook   978-1-4990-4439-3

Rev. date: 09/02/2014

To order additional copies of this book, contact:
Xlibris LLC
1-888-795-4274
www.Xlibris.com
Orders@Xlibris.com

CONTENTS

CHAPTER 1

Molina

The rays of sunlight began peeping through the branches of the forest trees. Molina sat up, stretching her small arms above her head. A big yawn spread across her pretty little face.

Molina's father walked in and said, "Good morning, Princess, are you ready to begin the day?"

"Oh yes, Father!" Molina replied.

Molina approached every day with the dream of leaving her small village and living in the Enchanted Kingdom. Her entire life had been filled with stories of the beautiful kingdom. She could close her eyes and hear the musical sounds of horse hooves dancing on the cobblestone streets. Birds tweeting their happy sounds and the laughter of children filling the walls of the city.

"Molina, where are you? You look like you have traveled to a place far, far away," her father said.

"Sorry, Father, I guess I was daydreaming again," Molina replied.

"Chop-chop, the morning is slipping away," her father cheered.

"Yes, Father."

Molina skipped down the dirt path leading to the old wooden barn. "Good morning, chickens," Molina sang. She knew her dream of moving to the Enchanted Kingdom was going to be through the gift these amazing chickens gave her every day.

The chickens were so excited to see Molina that they moved off their nests to show her their prize. Molina graciously removed each egg and carefully placed them in her cloth-lined basket. The blue-and-white checked fabric quickly disappeared below the delicate eggs. The chickens chirped with excitement knowing they were helping Molina fulfill her dream, which she shared with them daily.

Molina went into the kitchen, finding her mother kneading dough for their daily bread. She kissed her mom on her flour-covered cheek and then sneezed as the flour tickled her nose. "Bless you, my princess," her mother whispered in her daughter's ear.

"Good morning, Mother, how many eggs do we need to keep today?"

"Just six eggs should be good for this morning. How many did your magical chickens give you today?" her mother questioned.

"My goodness, Mother, can you believe they gave me thirty eggs? That's an all-time record!" Molina chimed with glee.

"Molina, it must be all the love you show them. I've never seen chickens produce like they do."

"Mother, may I go to my favorite spot to sell them?" Molina asked politely.

"Of course, sweetheart, just be careful of the horses," her mother replied sweetly.

Molina carefully removed six eggs and placed them in the red-and-white striped bowl next to her mother. She then set out to sell her magic eggs, whistling a tune as her little legs skipped her to the crossroads of town.

CHAPTER 2

The Crossroads

The crossroads was her favorite place to sell her eggs. She loved speaking to the travelers as they made their way past her to some exotic place. Their stories of their travels always fascinated her. The favorite destination of the people passing by was the Enchanted Kingdom.

When she arrived at the crossroads, she made herself comfortable on the trunk of a fallen tree. From here she could see the people coming from all directions. She sat ladylike on the tree trunk and placed her basket of eggs gingerly on her lap.

Molina's face lit up with the most infectious smile as she watched a traveler approach. "Good morning, young lady," said the traveler as he got closer. "You have the smile of a princess!"

"Good morning, sir. Would you like to buy some of the most magical eggs in the village?"

"What makes your eggs so magical?" the traveler inquired.

"The different-colored eggs have a different flavor. The pink ones have a hint of peppermint, the chocolate brown ones a touch of cocoa, and the tan eggs a little taste of vanilla. But more important than the taste, it is the sense of joy and happiness one feels after eating them. My mother says it is because of all the love and attention that I show my chickens." Molina gleamed with pride.

"Well, that sounds great, but your angelic smile already sold them. With a smile like yours, who could say no?" the man replied.

Molina asked, "So you want to buy some of the eggs?"

"But of course," said the traveler.

"How many do you want?"

"How many do you have?"

"Twenty-four eggs, sir."

"Then I think I will buy them all. I am traveling to the Enchanted Kingdom to sell other items, maybe they will fetch a good fare."

The traveler gave her a shiny gold coin.

"Thank you, sir!" Molina exclaimed with joy.

Molina took the coin and tucked it in her small white eyelet pocket. It was the most she had ever received for her eggs.

The traveler asked with a whimsical smile, "What is your name, my child?"

"I am Molina, sir, and one day I am going to travel to the Enchanted Kingdom to live!"

"Well, young lady, my name is Jean Paul, and I very often travel this route. If your eggs fetch what I think they will, I will buy from you again. Until next time, Molina, have a wonderful day."

Molina, so excited about her sale, skipped home with sheer excitement.

"Mother, Father, you won't believe—look what my chickens gave me today. This gold coin is from my sale of their twenty-four eggs. A very kind traveler named Jean Paul purchased them."

Molina's father kissed her forehead. "Molina, go and put your coin away in your safe hiding place. One day your hard work will take you to your dream."

"Yes, Father." And Molina went to hide her coin.

CHAPTER 3

As Dreams Come True

Time passed quickly, and the once-small child named Molina grew into a beautiful young woman. Each day started the same as it had for many years. The sun would rise over the tips of the trees, spilling their rays through her window. Molina would stretch her now-long arms above her head, reaching for the ceiling. Today, however, was different. Today was the first day of a new life, the beginning of a dream coming true. Molina, with outstretched arms, let a sleepy yawn fill her face, which quickly grew into a big smile.

Her father said, "Good morning, Princess! Are you ready? Today is the day."

Molina squealed, "Yes, Father, and today is the day!" She quickly dressed and ran to the barn.

"Good morning, chickens!" The chickens, so happy to see her, chirped uncontrollably. They had heard day after day her dreams of traveling to the Enchanted Kingdom, and now the day had come. Through their daily gift

to her, she had enough money to move to the Enchanted Kingdom. They were all so happy that they had laid more eggs than ever for her. She sang with happiness as she gathered their bounty.

Her mother and father were sad about her leaving but happy for her dream coming true. Her mother carefully packed her food and clothes for her move. The three of them walked to the crossroads to meet her friend and traveler Jean Paul.

Over the years, Jean Paul had watched this small child grow into a beautiful young woman. That day, her beauty was radiant. He knew that this small child was what had brought him his success. The eggs that he bought from her had magic qualities that brought him fame in the surrounding villages and kingdoms. Bakers in the Enchanted Kingdom began meeting him at the gates to buy the eggs.

Today would be the last purchase from Molina. They had become quite good friends over the years, and today he was the safe transport of Molina to the great city she had always dreamed of.

With her big blue eyes full of tears, she hugged her mother and father good-bye. She looked back as long as she could to watch her parents waving farewell. Soon the road turned, and the vision of her parents disappeared.

The road was bumpy, but the excitement of her destination far exceeded the discomfort. She was amazed at how gallantly Jean Paul handled the beautiful horses pulling the wagon. They talked without pause for hours. She loved the stories of the great places he had seen. His brown eyes twinkled as he wove his words into a wonderful fabric of fabled places.

Jean Paul listened and laughed at Molina's simple tales of the bartering women wanting the magic eggs with the hopes of not paying, offering a date with their son in exchange for an egg.

Soon the day disappeared, and the noises of the night filled her ears. The joyous sound of the crickets and owls and the bellowing of a wolf in the distance created a symphony of music.

As the night grew darker, the sky was suddenly filled with sparkles of light. The stars seemed to come to life as Jean Paul spoke of Orion's belt and the Small and Big Dipper.

Molina fell asleep to the lovely sound of Jean Paul's voice and the beautiful melody played by the creatures of the forest.

The next morning, Jean Paul greeted her with breakfast, and the two travelers began their journey. It took three more days to get to the kingdom. Molina's breath was taken away by the beauty of the city. The sun seemed to dance across the buildings. The merchants saw Jean Paul coming and

quickly greeted him. Molina was amazed at his popularity. She then realized that it was her magic eggs that they sought.

Jean Paul sold all the eggs quickly, selling them to the highest bidders. He turned to Molina and said, "My success is because of you, young lady." He took the coins he had collected and shared them with her.

Her face lit up with joy. Now she had enough money to live without worrying for a while. Between what she had saved before the journey and what Jean Paul had just shared, things were going to be a little easier.

Jean Paul helped her find a small, affordable room in the heart of the kingdom. They had dinner together, and then her friend walked her home and kissed her hand good-night.

The following day, Jean Paul left for his next adventure. Molina bid him farewell, and she knew she would miss him terribly.

All her life she had waited for this moment. Now that it was here, she didn't know what to do next. She decided to go out and explore the city. It was as amazing as she had dreamed. Although not actually diamonds, the roads did sparkle from the flecks in the cobblestone streets. The light seemed to bounce off the walls of the buildings, sending little rainbows dancing like butterflies through the air.

Molina was enjoying her life in the kingdom, although it was hard to meet friends. She filled her days exploring and her evenings dreaming of Jean Paul's return.

A month passed before Jean Paul's travels brought him back to the kingdom. Before his return, he stopped to purchase more eggs from Molina's parents. They filled his wagon with gifts for Molina including her favorite cookies and her mother's homemade bread. Upon his return to the kingdom he was met with Molina's enchanting smile. Jean Paul presented her with a magical white dove. The dove immediately replaced her loneliness with love.

Jean Paul was only there a few days before he left again. Molina was very sad about his departure. She realized that without friends and family, life was not perfect, even in an enchanted kingdom.

Molina had ridden to the gates of the city with Jean Paul and walked back quietly with her new white dove in her pocket.

CHAPTER 4

The Woman in Need

When Molina reached her apartment, an old beggar woman sat on the bottom step of the stairs. She was pleading with anyone passing by to help her. Molina was stunned by the indifference of everyone who saw her. Molina sat down beside the woman and took her hand in hers.

"My name is Molina, and I want to help you," she whispered to the woman.

The woman, barely able to speak, said, "Bless you, child," and collapsed in her arms.

Molina paid a young boy to help her take the woman to her apartment. The woman was hot to the touch. Molina did everything she remembered her mother doing for her when she was sick. She placed a cool rag on her head. She tried to get the woman to drink and eat.

Molina cared for the woman the best that she could, but the woman did not seem to be getting any better. Molina began to get scared for the woman's well-being, so she gathered all her money to seek proper medical help.

She walked to the open market, asking each vendor what to do. She finally found a potion maker to concoct a formula to help the old woman. Molina was excited to get back to her guest with the cure for her ailment. She was in such a rush she took a shortcut through an alley. Two boys her age had been watching her in the market. They followed Molina, and when they were out of sight of anyone passing by, they cornered her and stole the elixir and all her remaining money from her pocket. Her white dove took flight when they grabbed the pocket in which he was concealed.

Molina was left alone in the alley, devastated by the theft. She sat down on the dirty street, hugging her legs and placing her head to her knees, and began to cry. "How could this happen?" she spoke out loud. She did not care about the money; she only cared about the medicine that was now gone. How was she going to help her friend?

Suddenly her white dove returned with the most beautiful piece of silk she had ever seen. He gently dropped the silk in her lap and then crawled back into her pocket. She had an idea. She ran back to the medicine woman and begged for her to trade the silk for the medicine. The woman agreed, and Molina took the medicine and ran back to her apartment.

She sat with the woman night and day, but she did not seem to be getting better. Molina, not knowing who to turn to, gathered all her things and made a stretcher from two limbs of a fallen tree with her mother's blanket

sewn around the limbs. Early the next morning, she gently lifted the woman and placed her on the stretcher. The journey back home would be difficult, and Molina knew she had to move quickly.

Days went by, and Molina dragged the woman behind her on the stretcher. Occasionally a traveler would assist her for as long as possible before leaving them alone again.

As Molina approached the crossroads to her village, she collapsed from exhaustion. Her little white dove wiggled out of her pocket. He flew to Molina's parent's home. The bird entered the home through an open window. Her parents were shocked to see the bird. Could this be the same white dove that Jean Paul had shown them? If so, was Molina nearby? The bird kept flying in and out of the house. Molina's mother and father finally followed the bird. In the distance, Molina's father saw something in the road. He ran to the site and found Molina and the woman. He scooped up his little girl and began to cry. Her mother frantically started waving her arms high overhead to stop the traveler approaching the crossroads. When the horse-drawn wagon got close enough, Molina's mother yelled, "Jean Paul, come quick!"

Jean Paul hurried to them. He helped Molina's father with Molina and the old woman.

CHAPTER 5

The Return Home

Molina recovered first. Her exhaustion soon passed after a few days with her mother's home-cooked meals plus some much-needed sleep.

The old woman was not so lucky. She was so frail. Molina's parents helped every way they knew how. Molina refused to leave her side. Jean Paul would make trips to the kingdom looking for a magic cure.

It had been so long since Molina had been home. She had been so engrossed in helping her friend she had not even gone to see her chickens. This particular morning, she went out to the barn. The chickens were chirping with excitement, just like old times.

"Good morning, chickens," Molina said in a very sad voice. The chickens quieted down for they could hear the sadness in her voice. Molina began to cry. To the same chickens she had shared her dreams with, she was now sharing her pain. She shared the story of the old woman and how she did not care about her dream of living in the Enchanted Kingdom any more. She shared that she would give up her dream with no sorrow or regrets if

she could only help this woman, a friend, a stranger whose name she did not even know.

The usually noisy chickens sat in silence as they listened to Molina.

When Molina finally stopped to wipe the tears from her cheeks, one chicken moved off her nest to expose two perfect eggs. Molina took the eggs and thanked the chicken.

She left the barn and went to the kitchen. Her mother, covered in flour, looked at Molina and took her face in her hands and kissed her forehead.

Molina managed a small smile.

Molina took the heavy cast-iron skillet off the wall. She took a small square of butter and melted it in the skillet. She took the gift her chicken had given her and began scrambling the eggs. The delicious aroma was like nothing she or her mother had ever smelled before. The aroma wafted through the house. Molina put the eggs on a plate and went to feed her friend.

Molina was shocked to find the old woman sitting upright, frail but smiling.

"I just smelled the most wonderful food," the woman said in a quiet, wispy voice.

"Hi, I am Molina. It's so nice to see you up. May I ask your name?"

"My dear child, you will know soon enough," the woman said with a smile on her face.

Molina sat on her bed and fed the old woman the eggs.

Days passed, and the old woman continued to improve. She began walking with Molina and building her strength. Molina kept asking the woman what her name was, and the woman would always respond, "All in due time, my child."

One night at dinner, the woman announced that it was time to return to the Enchanted Kingdom.

Jean Paul offered his services, and she graciously accepted.

"My dear young man," she said with a scratchy voice, "I do not have any way of paying you."

Jean Paul replied, "My dear friend, it is not money I seek, it is your safe return to your home that I want. Molina has taught me the value of doing for others with no expectation of anything in return. I know my success has been because of this lesson from our sweet Molina."

The woman looked at Molina and said, "My sweet young friend, how can I ever repay you? You were cheated out of your dream by helping me, and yet you do not seem upset or disappointed. What can I ever do for you?"

Molina, with her angelic voice, replied, "Dreams change, sometimes what you seek turns out to be different than how you imagined them. The truth is the journey was the dream. If I had not dreamed about the Enchanted Kingdom, I would have never enjoyed collecting the eggs like I did. If I had not spent so much time with my chickens, they would have never produced like they did. If there were never any extra eggs, I would have never met my dearest friend, Jean Paul. Without Jean Paul, I would have never had the courage to move to the Enchanted Kingdom. You see, all these events took me to the spot where I met you. I know now my true destiny was to save you. My dream changed to something better—the dream of caring for someone else even if it meant sacrificing something I thought I wanted. Your health became my dream."

Her family sat in silence. Jean Paul and the woman had no idea how to respond to such an insight on life. The old woman, moved almost to tears by the sentiment, spoke in a very quiet voice, "My sweet Molina, my debt to you can never be repaid. I have never had anyone hold me in such high regard. My heart and soul had been even more stricken by illness than the physical disease you saved me from. You have healed me in more ways than you will ever know."

Molina looked the woman in her faint gray eyes and said, "You are part of me, you are a part of my family. Knowing you has brought me more than riches. My only wish for you is to stay healthy and live a happy life."

The woman bowed her head and said, "I owe you that, and I will make that my dream for myself. Thank you, Molina."

That night, those surrounding Molina fell asleep with joy in their hearts.

CHAPTER 6
Dreams Do Come True

Early the next morning as the sun began to rise over the treetops, Molina skipped to the barn like the child she once was.

"Good morning, chickens!" Molina sang.

The chickens could feel that happiness had returned to Molina's voice. They cackled with delight. She continued her conversation with her feathered friends about everything that had happened. Her friend had regained her health and was returning to her home in the Enchanted Kingdom. And she was as happy for her as she had been for herself when she set out on the same journey.

She gathered the abundance of eggs and headed toward her house. Her parents were helping Jean Paul and the woman prepare for the long journey home. Molina gave all the eggs to her friends. They all walked toward the crossroads. Conversation was quiet. Molina knew her life had changed its course. She said good-bye to Jean Paul and then turned to the woman and asked, "May I know your name now?"

She replied, "All in good time."

Jean Paul and the woman departed from the crossroads heading for the Enchanted Kingdom. Molina watched as they disappeared from sight. She wondered if the woman would have the same excitement she had on the journey. Her father put his arm around her as they walked home.

He said to her in a very choked voice, "I'm proud of you, my little princess. You put your own dreams and desires on hold to help someone in need. You could not have made me any prouder than I am right now."

"Thank you, Father, I learned that from you. The day I left I now know what you were feeling. You also put your dreams aside so I could live mine. I understand that now. I love you both for teaching me."

CHAPTER 7

Homeward Bound

The ride back to the Enchanted Kingdom was done in silence. Both travelers were awestruck by Molina. When they approached the Enchanted Kingdom, Jean Paul was greeted by a large group of store owners. With the flurry of business around his wagon, he never saw the old woman disappear in the crowd.

Weeks passed, and one morning, Molina was awakened not by the rays of sunlight but by the thundering hooves of horses. She quickly got dressed and ran outside. Her parents were already there. Molina stood in amazement by the horse-drawn carriage with six of the most beautiful white horses she had ever seen. The jewel-covered coach was driven by a regal man with plumes of feathers from his cap. His uniform was adorned by strands of gold. The deep-purple velvet was offset by the whitest of white fabric.

Twelve knights stood guard around the carriage. Their silver armor glistened in the sun. They stood perfectly still at complete attention.

Suddenly the carriage door opened, and a very handsome man a little older than Molina stepped out. He gently held out his hand to assist the passenger. A beautiful woman appeared as he gracefully helped her down.

"Hello, Molina," the man said.

Confused, Molina responded, "Hello."

The voice was not as deep or raspy, but the eyes she definitely knew. They were the eyes of Jean Paul.

The woman looked at Molina and said, "Hello, my sweet Molina."

Molina grew weak in the knees, and her father grabbed her elbow to steady her.

"My dear Molina, I said I would tell you my name in due time. My name is Queen Annabelle. I am the queen of the Enchanted Kingdom. My son and I have been on a journey for over a decade looking for goodness. An opportunity came to us to improve our Kingdom. A chance to get a glimpse of what life is like for a person less fortunate, a person not born into privilege in the kingdom. A chance to see life from a different perspective, identify what is wrong in our society, and make changes to make our kingdom stronger. We both drank a potion that would age us and change our physical attributes to disguise our true identities. The only way to break the spell was to find true kindness. Jean Paul and I both believed when

we drank that potion that we would find this kind of goodness quickly in the Enchanted Kingdom. We both grew weary on this quest. Jean Paul began looking outside the kingdom, and this is when he met you. His encounter with you gave him hope, and he returned to tell me. You were but a small child. Jean Paul knew you were the one. We, however, continued our search, and in the process, I began to lose faith that there was anyone with this kind of goodness left. Jean Paul's health stayed strong because of his continued visits with you. I, however, continued to weaken from the disappointment in my people in the Enchanted Kingdom. They had been showered by the wealth and prosperity of the kingdom, but their souls had become poor. You, Molina, possess what I want to restore in the kingdom. You cherish a person's life over the things that we acquire."

Jean Paul's eyes were transfixed on Molina. For years he had loved her sweetness and goodness. Jean Paul kneeled down in front of her and took a ring from his pocket.

"Molina, I have loved you since I met you. I could not reveal who I really was, but I knew you were the one. The one to break the spell, the one to restore the kingdom, the one I want to continue to learn from for the rest of my life."

"Marry me, Molina, and complete my soul."

Molina's father shook her elbow to break the trance she seemed to be in.

Molina nodded, still unable to speak.

The two families celebrated the engagement with their favorite food, scrambled eggs and fresh bread.

Jean Paul and Queen Annabelle helped Molina's family pack up all their possessions, including the chickens. Molina and her parents moved into the castle with the royal family.

The whole kingdom participated in the royal wedding. Gifts were delivered daily to the castle. Their decision of what to do with the gifts was easy due to the valuable lesson the queen and her son learned from the spell. Molina and her parents went out to the people of the kingdom and shared the gifts with those in need. Through the distribution of gifts, Molina heard many stories of unfortunate families in need. One such story was of a family of children who had lost both parents. Molina and her parents set out to find the eight orphaned children.

When Molina found the children, they were thrilled with the gifts she shared. Two of the children kept their heads low, concealing their eyes from Molina. When she addressed the two of them, only one looked up. She realized he was one of the boys that robbed her. He looked frightened as he looked into her eyes. Molina moved closer to the boy and then reached out to hug him. She reassured the clan that they would never be hungry again. She bestowed forgiveness on the two boys. Molina realized

that their actions had not been for greed but for survival. She vowed that these children were now part of her and her family. The fear of survival was quickly replaced with hope and jubilation.

Through the spell, everyone would benefit. At the wedding of Jean Paul and Molina, the queen stood before her people and shared her experience. Some of her people bowed their heads in shame for they had been the ones who ignored the old woman in need. Her message was crystal clear to everyone. The kingdom would only be as wealthy as the poorest son or daughter. "We must care for one another in order to keep the kingdom strong!" she proclaimed.

From that day forward, the story of Molina spread from the gates of the Enchanted Kingdom through the countryside. The kingdom gained strength each day that passed. Days became years, and years became centuries, but the story of Molina never faded. It is the powerful tale of how one peasant child altered the history of a kingdom.

Edwards Brothers Malloy
Thorofare, NJ USA
October 31, 2014